JAMES THURBER'S

Many Moons

DRAMATIZED

BY

CHARLOTTE B. CHORPENNING

THE DRAMATIC PUBLISHING COMPANY

Many Moons

A Play in Three Acts
FOR TEN CHARACTERS

"Many Moons"* was originally produced by *The Hessville Children's Theatre, Hessville, Indiana,* under the direction of *Laura M. Hall,* with scenery and lighting by *Nora MacAlvay.* The entire cast was made up of sixth grade children, with the exception of a fifth grade boy who played the part of the Jester.

CYNICIA, the Chamberlain's wife............Lucille Snyder
ROYAL NURSE ....Darlene Socks
LORD HIGH CHAMBERLAIN...........Gordon Ellinghausen
ROYAL WIZARD ....Kenneth Marquiss
PARETTA, the Wizard's wife................Patricia Kelly
MATHEMATICIAN ....Ronald Edmonds
JESTER ....Joe Heggi
PRINCESS LENORE ....Lorraine Heresz
KING ....Kenneth Crowe
GOLDSMITH'S DAUGHTER ....Sylvia Roberts

SYNOPSIS

ACT ONE: *A room in the palace. Toward evening, once upon a time.*

ACT TWO: *The throne room. The next afternoon.*

ACT THREE: *The Princess' bedroom. Moonrise, the same night.*

*This play is the only dramatization of the story to be performed in the non-professional (amateur) theatre. Suggestions for the production of this play will be found at the end of the text.

ACT ONE

SCENE: *A room in the palace. One door, back, left of center, leads to the Princess' bedroom above. If the play is done in curtains, they may be looped back, with a backing, or merely pushed aside as the actors exit through a break in the curtains. If a complete setting is used, it is effective, though not necessary, to have the door wide enough to show the beginning of a marble staircase. Actors turning left as they go through the door, go to the garden; turning right, they go to the Goldsmith's shop; straight back, they go up the stairs. Another door, down right, leads to the Wisemen's quarters. There is a tall window, left, a little more than half way down. It may be shown by drawing back the curtains part way, at a break in them, or built into the set. Five bell cords hang near the corner, right, back. A long, narrow table with a cloth hanging to the floor stands parallel with the footlights, about a third of the distance back. Against it, front, slightly right of center, is a bench. Another bench is down left, against the wall. A high-backed chair, with royal insignia at the top, and arms on either side, stands back of the table, about a fourth of the way from end to end. It has been pushed back when the Princess slid out of it, so it stands sideways a little. In front of it, on the table, is a plate holding a broken tart. At the other end of the table is a high pyramid of tarts on a platter. Back of it are three separate,*

5

practical tarts, which do not show. An additional chair or two may be added if desired, but are not needed in the action.]

AT RISE OF CURTAIN: *The stage is empty. It is toward evening.* CYNICIA *enters, down right, goes to the Princess' chair, is shocked to find it empty, and hurries to pull a bell cord—three long pulls and one short one. Before she finishes, the* ROYAL NURSE *enters, back, in haste, carrying a large thermometer. She throws up her hands in alarm when she sees the empty chair.*]

NURSE

Where is the Princess? I came to take her temperature.

CYNICIA

We left her here, eating tarts.

NURSE

She has no appetite at all, any more. Where did she go?

CYNICIA

I don't know.

NURSE [*at the window*]

She isn't in the garden. The King is there alone. He's waving his arms about and bumping into things.

CYNICIA

He's beside himself because the Princess is so ill.

NURSE

I must find her! It's way past time to take her temperature and look at her tongue. Suppose she's walking in her sleep again! She might fall into the fountain in the garden!

[*The* NURSE *hurries off, back, turning left, to the garden.* CYNICIA *looks out the other door, impatiently, and then examines the pyramid of tarts. Then she picks up the broken*

*one in front of the Princess' chair and puts it down with a
shake of her head. The* LORD HIGH CHAMBERLAIN *enters,
down right. He bows, then checks himself, half up, in surprise.*]

CHAMBERLAIN

Your Majesty——Wife! That was the King's bell for me—
three long pulls and one short.

CYNICIA

I knew you'd come at once if you thought it was the King.

CHAMBERLAIN

What have I done now?

CYNICIA [*pointing to the empty chair*]

It's what you haven't done.

CHAMBERLAIN [*gasping*]

Where is the Princess?

CYNICIA

Take off those glasses when you talk to me. They make your
eyes look twice as large as they really are. That makes you
look twice as wise as you really are.

CHAMBERLAIN

I am the Lord High Chamberlain. I ought to look wise.

CYNICIA

Don't widen your eyes like that! It makes you look four
times as wise as you really are!

CHAMBERLAIN

It makes the King look up to me.

CYNICIA

It makes the King order you to get things that are four times
too hard for you to get.

CHAMBERLAIN [*very pompous*]

I have sent very far away to get things for the King.

CYNICIA

I know! You feel eight times as wise as you really are. But you're not wise enough to get the Princess the kind of tarts the King ordered you to get.

CHAMBERLAIN

The King said to me, "The Princess has lost her appetite. She is very fond of raspberry tarts. Get her all she wants. They will bring back her appetite, and she will not be ill any more." She has eaten many tarts already. [*He points to the pyramid on the table.*] I have got her a great many more.

CYNICIA

And you never thought to ask him what kind of raspberries you should put in them.

CHAMBERLAIN

I did ask him that. He said, "Get her any kind her heart desires."

CYNICIA

And you haven't got her that kind. At first she ate them eagerly. Then she had to be coaxed to eat them. And now— [*She points to the empty chair.*]—you haven't found out yet what kind she wants! The Court Jester will come bounding in here any minute. He'll find out what kind the Princess wants. He'll tell the King. What will the King think of you then?

CHAMBERLAIN [*taking off his glasses, deflated*]

I've done my best. I've got her red raspberries, and black raspberries, and yellow raspberries, and green raspberries, and rubos strigosus, and rubos occidentalis——

CYNICIA

What good is your best when you feel wiser than you really are?

[*The* ROYAL WIZARD *enters, down right, with* PARETTA, *his wife. The* WIZARD *carries a potion in a little bottle.*]

WIZARD

I came to ask whether the Princess——

PARETTA [*finishing his sentence*]

——is feeling better.

WIZARD [*irritated*]

That is not what I was going to say! —whether she wanted one of those. [*He points to the pyramid of tarts.*]

CHAMBERLAIN

She went away and left them all.

WIZARD

That is what I feared. I brought her——

PARETTA

——sand from the sandman, to put her to sleep.

WIZARD [*about to explode*]

I am the Royal Wizard! Is it too much to ask of you, Wife, not to finish my sentences before you know——

PARETTA [*beaming*]

——what you were going to say?

WIZARD [*glaring*]

What I have brought is a potion to cure heartbreak. The Princess is very sad. The tears roll down her cheeks.

CYNICIA

The Princess is sad because the Lord High Chamberlain hasn't got her what her heart desires. She doesn't need potions. She needs the right kind of raspberry tarts.

CHAMBERLAIN [*pointing to the pyramid*]

One of those must be the right kind, but I can't get the Princess to taste another one.

[*The* ROYAL MATHEMATICIAN *enters, down right, carrying a long scroll which hangs nearly to his feet. He has pencils behind each ear.*]

MATHEMATICIAN

Did you find out what kind the Princess wanted?

[*The* OTHERS *shake their heads and point to the empty chair.*]

CHAMBERLAIN

She turned away her head. She wouldn't even look at them.

MATHEMATICIAN

I have here a list of every kind of raspberry tart that can be made or imagined. Let us make sure that every one of them is there, ready for the Princess.

CHAMBERLAIN [*pulling a list from his pocket*]

Let the Royal Mathematician read, and we will check on my list of what is piled up there.

CYNICIA

Be quick about it or the Court Jester will come bounding in and find out what kind the Princess wants so much it makes her ill—before you do.

CYNICIA *and* PARETTA [*together*]

What will the King think of you then?

[*The* MATHEMATICIAN *gives each a pencil, and they* ALL *bend over the lists with pencils ready. A faint tinkle comes from offstage. They* ALL *lift their heads.*]

CYNICIA

Is that the Jester's bells I hear?

MATHEMATICIAN

It is. He's coming here.

WIZARD

The Court Jester does not belong in serious business like this.

CYNICIA

He has the most illogical way of just—*jumping*—at conclusions that are right.

CHAMBERLAIN

Without sending anywhere to find out.

MATHEMATICIAN

Without adding or subtracting or computing, at all.

PARETTA

His mind works too fast.

WIZARD

He just turns things inside out.

CHAMBERLAIN

He just turns them upside down.

CYNICIA

It isn't fair to the Royal Wisemen. It makes them seem stupid.

MATHEMATICIAN

The King's court is no place for a leapfrog mind.

[*The* NURSE *enters, back, supporting the* PRINCESS, *who is hardly able to walk. There is a faraway, wistful smile on her face. The* WISEMEN *anxiously set the chair straight and lift her into it.*]

NURSE

I found her lying by a flower the gardner's scythe had missed when he mowed down the grass in the far corner of the garden.

PRINCESS [*faintly*]

I liked it.

NURSE

Bring her a tart. She must have——

PARETTA

—food.

[*The* CHAMBERLAIN *eagerly offers the* PRINCESS *a tart, but she turns away her head.*]

NURSE [*looking at her watch*]

Eat it like a good girl. In ten minutes I'll come to take your temperature again.

PRINCESS [*protesting*]

You did it in the garden.

NURSE

I must do it every so often.

[*The* NURSE *goes out, back. The* PRINCESS *lifts up the tart, shudders, lays it down again, leans back, and closes her eyes.*]

PRINCESS

Everyone makes me feel worse.

[*The* MATHEMATICIAN *motions toward the lists at the other end of the table, and the five of them gather to begin checking in silence. They are hardly settled to their work when the jingle of bells comes again, much nearer. They lift their heads and listen as it draws nearer.*]

CYNICIA

There he comes. I told you so.

[*The* COURT JESTER *bounds in, back, in his motley and his cap and his bells, and kneels at the* PRINCESS' *side.*]

PRINCESS [*opening her eyes, with a wan smile, extending her hand for him to kiss*]

It's my dear funny Jester.

JESTER

I was playing with the unicorn in the forest, and all of a sudden it seemed to me that the Princess had need of me. What can I do for your Royal Highness?

PRINCESS [*still weak*]

I want you to make me laugh, of course, silly.

[*The* JESTER *leaps to his feet and lays his lute on the table.*]

JESTER

I saw two rabbits dancing on the shore when the dawn came up from the sea. They were trying to dance like the people in the palace, but every once in a while one would forget and hop like a rabbit or pound on the ground with his hind legs. If the Wisemen will clap the time, I'll show you.

CYNICIA

Wisemen do not clap for jesters' nonsense.

JESTER

Laughing isn't nonsense.

PRINCESS

I'll clap for you.

JESTER

It goes like this.

[*The* JESTER *sets the rhythm, clapping, and the* PRINCESS *takes it up. He leaps and scurries about, sometimes on two feet, sometimes on all fours.* Before the dance has gone on*

*See note on "The Rabbit Dance" at the end of the play.

very long, the PRINCESS' *strength begins to fail. Her clap-*
ping grows faint, slows, and she leans back and closes her
eyes, with a sigh. The JESTER *stands still, looking at her.*
The group at the other end of the table nod to each other,
pleased that he has failed.]

JESTER [*deeply concerned*]

There's no laugh left in her.

WIZARD

That should teach you not to meddle with things——

PARETTA

——you don't understand.

WIZARD [*glaring at his wife*]

——that are none of your business!

JESTER

The Princess is sad. It seemed to me that is my business.

MATHEMATICIAN

Yours! Can you compute the distance between a laugh and a
tear?

[*The* JESTER *backs away from the* PRINCESS, *slowly, his face*
and body taking on her expression and posture.]

JESTER

She wants something very much.

[*The* JESTER *watches the* PRINCESS *intently, sometimes even*
closing his eyes for an instant, as she has. The WIZARD *nods*
at him, jogging the CHAMBERLAIN'S *elbow.*]

WIZARD

He's got that far-off, find-out look.

CYNICIA

He'll jump to a conclusion, next we know.

MATHEMATICIAN

Without even a list.

CHAMBERLAIN

Or check marks, or——

PARETTA

—anything.

WIZARD

He'll tell the King.

CYNICIA *and* PARETTA [*in one breath*]

What will the King think of you then?

WISEMEN

Sh-h-h-h! . . .

CYNICIA

He doesn't hear. He's listening to himself.

PARETTA [*pushing the* WIZARD]

Go on. Make her tell.

CYNICIA [*pushing the* CHAMBERLAIN]

Get ahead of him.

[*The three* WISEMEN *go to the* PRINCESS. *They are confused at the sight of her still face and form. The* WIZARD *takes off his hat and stares into it. The* MATHEMATICIAN *takes his pencils from behind his ears and stares at them. The* CHAMBERLAIN *wipes his forehead with a big handkerchief. They look at each other and at* CYNICIA *and* PARETTA.]

CYNICIA *and* PARETTA [*together*]

Go on. Ask her.

[*The* WIZARD *mutters into his cap. The* MATHEMATICIAN *walks around in little circles. The* CHAMBERLAIN *blows his nose loudly.*]

WIZARD

Abacadabra, abacadabra!

MATHEMATICIAN [*counting rapidly*]

One, two, three, four, five.

[*The* PRINCESS *opens her eyes at the sounds.*]

CHAMBERLAIN

Princess Lenore, what kind is it you want so much it makes you ill?

PRINCESS

I don't know. I want some kind of—of——

PARETTA

—tarts.

[*The* WISEMEN *and* CYNICIA *snap their heads toward* PARETTA *and correct her in soft fury.*]

WISEMEN *and* CYNICIA

Raspberries!

PRINCESS [*not heeding them*]

—of something. The feeling comes up in me the way the tides come up in the sea. But I don't know what it is I want.

CHAMBERLAIN

How can you want it when you don't know what it is?

PRINCESS

I don't know. Do you think I could be keeping secrets from myself?

[*The* JESTER *bounds to the end of the table, silently, and leans toward the* PRINCESS.]

JESTER

Try to tell yourself your secret, Princess. Think about what you want.

PRINCESS [*looking at the tarts with a little shudder*]

I have thought.

JESTER

You've thought about what you didn't want. Now think about what you do want.

CYNICIA

If you find out, the Wisemen will get it for you.

PRINCESS

Oh, do you think they can?

CHAMBERLAIN

Of course!

MATHEMATICIAN

We are the Royal Wisemen!

WIZARD

We get the King anything he wants.

CHAMBERLAIN

No matter how far we have to send to get it.

WIZARD

The Royal Mathematician has made a list. Just listen and shake your head "no" if it isn't the one you want.

JESTER

The Princess is too ill for that. It's very tiring to keep shaking your head "no." I think she should shake her head "yes," if it *is* the one she wants.

MATHEMATICIAN

You think! Can you figure the distance between wanting something and getting it?

PRINCESS

Read me your list. I'll shake my head "yes," if you come to it. [*She leans back and closes her eyes.*]

CHAMBERLAIN

Leave out the ones she's tried already. They are checked off with a little check mark.

[*The* CHAMBERLAIN *reads very fast, and the* MATHEMATICIAN *draws lines across the items on his list.*]

CHAMBERLAIN [*reading*]

Red, black, yellow, green, strigosus, occidentalis; wild, from the slopes of Parnassus; canned, from a farm in Ohio; frozen, from the layer of eternal ice in Siberia; big ones grown in a hothouse; little ones blighted by frost in the spring; sweetened with sugar—white sugar, brown sugar, maple sugar; sweetened with honey——

JESTER

Has she eaten all of those?

CHAMBERLAIN

She's tasted every single one.

JESTER

It's a good many. Do you suppose——

MATHEMATICIAN

We don't suppose. We count.

WIZARD

And conjure.

CHAMBERLAIN

And check.

CYNICIA

Now listen carefully, Princess, for the one you want.

CHAMBERLAIN [*reading, but not so fast*]

Dried raspberries, dug from a buried city in the island of Crete; water-soaked, washed up by the tides from the kingdom under the sea——

[*The* PRINCESS *opens her eyes.*]

PRINCESS

I'd like to see that one.

[*The* JESTER *grows more intent.*]

CHAMBERLAIN

That's one the Royal Wizard thought up. He'll have to get on his flying-carpet and bring it to you.

WIZARD

The flying-carpet——

PARETTA

—doesn't work.

WIZARD [*demolishing her with his eyes*]

—flies in the air like a bird. It doesn't swim in the water like a fish.

MATHEMATICIAN

Anyway, there's no such thing as a kingdom under the sea.

PRINCESS [*sitting up, her face alight*]

There must be. I've seen the path to it shining on the sea.

[*The* JESTER *slips to the window and looks out.*]

MATHEMATICIAN [*very positive*]

The sea has seventy-one million squares miles. It is four miles deep. There is enough salt in it to put on the tails of— well, I'll have to figure out how many birds. That is all there is to the sea.

JESTER

It has tides.

[*The* PRINCESS *sits back, listless, and closes her eyes.*]

PRINCESS

Go on.

CHAMBERLAIN [*reading*]

Raspberries picked in the shade—in the sun—in the rain—in the dark, in the darkest Africa—under the moon in Mandalay——

[*The* PRINCESS *sits up.*]

PRINCESS

Let me see that one.

CHAMBERLAIN

That one isn't in the pile. But if it is the one you want, the Wizard will put on his seven-league boots and bring it to you.

PRINCESS

I don't know whether it is or not.

WIZARD

Think about it. Think hard.

JESTER

Shut your eyes and listen to yourself. Maybe you will tell yourself your secret.

PRINCESS

Go away, all of you. I'll try.

[*The* PRINCESS *wrinkles up her brow in an effort to think. The* WISEMEN *and* CYNICIA *and* PARETTA *go to the end of the table where the pyramid of tarts rests, and work over the* lists, quietly. *The* JESTER *leans to murmur in the* PRINCESS' *ear.*]

JESTER

Under the moon, in Mandalay . . .

[*Gradually, the* PRINCESS *relaxes. The* JESTER *picks up his lute and goes to lean against the window, watching her. A slow smile grows on her face. Soft music—"Moonlight Sonata"—rises gradually to fill the air. The group at the end of the table do not hear it, for they continue their checking, undisturbed. The* JESTER *does hear it, for he lifts a listening face. He picks up his lute, which he had stood against the wall, puts it to his ear, and sets it down; it does not come from there. He looks ahead, rejecting them as the source, utterly. He steals to the* PRINCESS, *puts his head close to hers, and is satisfied. He sets the lute on the end of the table, near her, shakes a finger at it, and leans over to whisper to it. He goes to sit on the bench in front of the table, where he can watch the* PRINCESS *and copy her movements and expressions. The* PRINCESS *is seeing pictures in her mind. Her attitudes and movements show clearly when they change and where they appear to her—at one side or the other, in front, below her, etc., and her wonder, surprise, delight, etc., at what she sees. Since she is seeing the same things the* JESTER *sees later, it may help the actress to learn his lines and think them to herself. The pictures are spaced to fit changes in the music. The* NURSE *bustles into the room, back.*]

NURSE [*briskly*]

It's time to take your temperature.

[EVERYONE *looks up with a start. The music fades away.*]

PRINCESS

Sh-h-h-h-h—you make it go away.

NURSE [*in great alarm*]

She's out of her head! What goes away?

PRINCESS

My secret was singing to me.

NURSE

Were any of you singing?

[*The* OTHERS *shake their heads, "no."*]

PRINCESS

It wasn't that sort of singing. It was inside my own self.

NURSE

Ringing in the ears!

PRINCESS

I was walking on a shining path. It led to——

PARETTA

——the kingdom under——

[PARETTA *is checked by hands over her mouth (her husband's). The* PRINCESS *continues, not noticing.*]

PRINCESS

——places I had never seen before. There was a magic sort of light over them.

NURSE

Delirium! Here—[*She thrusts a thermometer at the* PRINCESS.]—open your mouth. [*She puts it in the* PRINCESS' *mouth.*] Now, close it. [*She takes her wrist and counts the pulse.*] One—two—three . . . the pulse is weak. She must have food. Bring her a tart.

CHAMBERLAIN

We don't know what kind she wants.

NURSE

Never mind. She must have nourishment.

[*The* WISEMEN *each hold a tart before the* PRINCESS. *She turns her head away. The* JESTER *bounds to the end of the table.*]

JESTER

Royal Nurse! Royal Wisemen! It seems to me it isn't tarts the Princess wants—not any kind at all.

NURSE [*waving the* JESTER *away*]

Stick out your tongue. Dear me! . . . Very bad. . . . [*She takes a tart from the one nearest her.*] Eat this.

[*The* PRINCESS *moans and rests her head on her arms, on the arms of the chair. The* JESTER *whirls on them.*]

JESTER

If what the Princess wants so much it makes her ill and you keep making her eat tarts, something terrible will happen in the end!

MATHEMATICIAN

What do you know about it? Have you ever sent to the end of the endless?

JESTER

I say, if you keep giving her the wrong thing forever——

MATHEMATICIAN

You say! Can you compute where forever starts and stops?

JESTER

There isn't any sense in more tarts!

WIZARD

Sense, you say! Can you conjure sense out of the senseless?

[*The* WISEMEN *laugh, derisively.*]

JESTER

Didn't you hear what she said about her secret? It was singing to her. About a shining path across the sea. About a
magic sort of light. That's the sort of thing she wants! You
ought to find out what it is!

PRINCESS [*lifting her head*]

Talk some more.

NURSE

Quiet! You're disturbing the Princess. You're interfering
with the Royal Wisemen. The Princess is very ill. She must
take to her bed. [*She turns to* PARETTA.] Tell the King.
[*She turns to* CYNICIA.] You must help me carry her up the
marble staircase. The Wisemen must stay here and find out
what to do.

JESTER

There are forty-one wide marble steps. Let me help carry her.

NURSE

Out of the way!

[PARETTA *goes out, back.* CYNICIA *and the* NURSE *make a
chair out of their crossed hands, or support her otherwise,
and carry the* PRINCESS *off, back, and up the stairs. The*
JESTER *gives her a broken-hearted little wave.*]

JESTER

Good-bye.

PRINCESS [*with a wan smile, waving a weak hand*]

Good-bye.

[*The* JESTER *sits front, down left, on the bench, communing deeply with himself. The* WISEMEN *draw to the other end of the table. The* CHAMBERLAIN *removes his glasses and taps his forehead thoughtfully.*]

CHAMBERLAIN

Do you think—[*He jerks a thumb at the* JESTER.]—he's done it again?

MATHEMATICIAN

He's jumped to the right conclusion.

WIZARD

She doesn't want raspberry tarts, at all.

MATHEMATICIAN

We should have thought of that.

CHAMBERLAIN

Now that I look back, I can see it plainly.

WIZARD

Places she'd never seen before . . .

MATHEMATICIAN

A shining path on the water . . .

CHAMBERLAIN

That's the sort of thing she wants.

WIZARD

What can be the far-away, shining thing she wants?

MATHEMATICIAN

How far off is it?

WIZARD

What makes it shine?

CHAMBERLAIN

How far must I send to get it?

MATHEMATICIAN [*nodding toward the* JESTER]

He's got that look.

WIZARD

He jumped at what it isn't. Now, he'll jump at what it is.

CHAMBERLAIN

He'll tell the King.

MATHEMATICIAN

The King will order us to get it.

WIZARD

He'll say, "Get it tonight, tomorrow at the latest."

CHAMBERLAIN

He always does. He has no patience.

WIZARD

What shall we do if it's something we can't get so fast?

CHAMBERLAIN

We must remind him of all we've done for him already.

MATHEMATICIAN

We must each make a list of what we have done and have it ready in our pockets.

WIZARD

We can make up a few extra ones to put in.

CHAMBERLAIN

What if he says he doesn't remember them?

MATHEMATICIAN

We'll tell him he forgot.

WIZARD

Then he'll feel ashamed before us, his Wisemen.

MATHEMATICIAN

He'll talk out loud when he's alone, to keep from remembering that he forgot.

CHAMBERLAIN

And he'll understand how very wise we are.

[*The* WISEMEN *draw themselves up, feeling very wise and important. They hurry off, down right. The* JESTER *bounds up to shake a fist after them.*]

JESTER

You'll never be wise till you know that you aren't. [*He whirls around the stage, beating his hands together.*] What is it the Princess wants? What's shining in places she has never seen?

[*A sudden thought occurs to the* JESTER. *He stares at the Princess' chair, nods, sets the lute on the table, and shakes a finger at it.*]

JESTER

Play it to me. I want to see the pictures she was seeing.

[*The* JESTER *climbs into the chair, takes the positions she had, and presently makes the same motions she made, at the same places in the music.*]

JESTER [*in wonder*]

It must be Mandalay! There's a sort of magic light. Palm trees—and a temple with shining pillars—and people not like us. [*He gives an exclamation of surprise, at a picture he sees at one side and a little up.*] Oh-h! A wolf! On the edge of a mountain! He's lifting up his head and howling to the sky. [*He sees another picture, a little below him.*] A city— with a thousand roofs—maybe ten thousand! With a kind of glory over all of them, and people way down, running around like ants. [*He gives a laugh of delight, as a new picture appears, higher, to one side.*] Oh-oh! Little men, all dressed in fur! They crack their whips at the dogs that draw their sleds over the sparkling ice and snow! [*He sees an-*

other change.] Oh, my! Camels, carrying men with turbans over miles and miles of bright sand! [*He senses a mystery at the next picture, ahead of him, and seeming far away.*] An island. The ocean shimmers all around it till it meets the sky. [*He gets excited.*] Pirates are digging for buried treasure in the shadow of a tree! [*He sees another picture.*] Why! There's the shining path to the kingdom under the sea! It looks like——[*He sits up, popeyed.*] I've seen that path! I saw it from that window, just last night! [*He jumps down and bounds to the window.*] There it is now! It leads to—— [*He rushes to the door, back.*] Princess! Princess!

[*The* JESTER *goes out, back, and up the stairs, still calling. Before the sound has quite faded, the* KING *enters, back, steeped in gloom. He bumps into a chair on entering and throws out his hands in desperate grief.*]

KING [*very loud*]

Where is my Court Jester?

[*The* KING *strides to the bell cords, bumping again on the way. He pulls the jingling Jester's bell furiously. Then he crosses back to the pyramid of tarts and sinks onto the bench in front of the table, the picture of despair. The* JESTER* bounds into the room, back, and sits at the* KING'S *feet.*]

JESTER

What can I do for your Majesty?

KING

Nobody can do anything for me. The Princess is crying so much it makes her ill, and nobody can find out what she is crying for. There is nothing you can do for me except to play on your lute. Something sad.

[*The* JESTER *whispers to his lute, and the music rises softly. He listens to it intently.*]

KING [*impatiently*]

Why don't you play?

JESTER

I'm thinking about the Princess. What do your Wisemen say?

KING

They say it will take much counting and conjuring and sending to far places to find out what she wants. Meantime, she grows weaker all the time.

JESTER

Who knew all the time the Princess didn't want more tarts? It was the Princess herself. Perhaps she has found out what it is she wants by now. I will go and ask her.

[*The* JESTER *bounds to the door, back, just in time to meet the* PRINCESS *who enters, ready to fall from weakness. He leaps to catch her wavering form.*]

PRINCESS

I thought I heard you call.

JESTER

I did call.

PRINCESS

You sounded glad.

JESTER

I was glad. I saw your shining path to the sea. I thought if you looked at it you could tell the King what it is you want so much it makes you ill.

[*The* JESTER *leads the* PRINCESS *to the window. She follows the path with a pointing finger.*]

KING [*as the* PRINCESS *goes to the window*]

   I will get you anything your heart desires. Is there anything your heart desires?

PRINCESS [*in ecstasy*]

   That is what I was crying for. [*She goes to the* KING, *looking up at him piteously.*] I want the moon. If I can have the moon, I will be well again.

KING

   I have wonderful Wisemen who always get me anything I want. They will get it for me. You may have the moon.

PRINCESS [*leaning against the* KING]

   Then I will be well again.

CURTAIN

ACT TWO

SCENE: *The King's throne room. The doors and window may be left as in Act One, or they may be reversed. (Directions in this act place the entrances in the same positions as Act One; change accordingly.) The table is removed. A dais for the throne is desirable, though not necessary. The throne may be the same chair as used for the Princess in Act One, or another more elaborate one. It must have a royal insignia on the back. It stands on the side opposite the window, diagonally across a corner. The bench used in front of the table in Act One stands left (right, if the stage is reversed) of the dias and farther front, almost center stage. The bench against the wall, down left, remains. Other chairs are placed as desired.]*

AT RISE OF CURTAIN: *It is afternoon, the next day. The* KING *is pacing back and forth, serene, not bumping into anything. He goes, smiling, to pull the Chamberlain's bell. Before he has finished his three long and one short pulls, the* ROYAL NURSE *enters, back.]*

NURSE

Your Majesty, the Princess is getting restless. Tears roll down her cheeks again. She says, "When will my father bring me the moon?"

KING

Tell her tonight—tomorrow at the latest. I am seeing to it now.

NURSE

I hope that will quiet her.

[The NURSE goes out, back. The KING sits on his throne, spreading his train, settling his crown, smiling contentedly. The CHAMBERLAIN enters, down right, adjusting his glasses, widening his eyes, secure in his sense of importance.]

KING

I want you to get the moon. The Princess Lenore wants the moon. If she can have the moon, she will be well again.

CHAMBERLAIN *[shaken out of his pose]*

The moon?

KING

Yes, the moon. M-o-o-n—moon. Get it tonight. Tomorrow at the latest.

[The CHAMBERLAIN wipes his forehead and blows his nose loudly. He recovers his composure and begins to impress the KING, as he had planned.]

CHAMBERLAIN

I have got a great many things for you in my time, your Majesty. It just happens that I have with me a list of the things I have got for you in time. *[He pulls a long scroll of parchment out of his pocket and glances at it, frowning.]* Let me see, now. I have got—*[He reads.]*—"ivory, apes, and peacocks; rubies, opals, and emeralds; black orchids, pink elephants, blue poodles, and goldbugs; scarabs and flies in amber, hummingbirds' tongues, angels' feathers and unicorns' horns; giants, midgets, and mermaids; frankincense, ambergris, and myrrh; troubadours, minstrels, and dancing women;

a pound of butter, two dozen eggs, and a sack of sugar——"
Sorry, my wife wrote that in there.

KING

I don't remember any blue poodles.

CHAMBERLAIN

It says "blue poodles" right here on the list, and they are checked off with little check marks. So there must have been blue poodles. You just forgot.

KING [*hastily, bumping his hand on the arm of his chair as he gestures*]

Never mind the blue poodles. What I want now is the moon.

CHAMBERLAIN

I have sent as far as Samarkand and Araby and Zanzibar to get things for you, your Majesty. But the moon is out of the question. It is thirty-five thousand miles away and it is bigger than the room the Princess lies in. Furthermore, it is made of molten copper. I cannot get the moon for you. Blue poodles, yes; the moon, no.

KING [*getting to his feet in fury*]

You call yourself a wise man! Leave my presence! Send the Royal Wizard to the throne room.

[*The* CHAMBERLAIN *takes off his glasses and goes out, down right, rolling up his list, his head hanging. The* KING *strides about, bumping into things.*]

KING

Lord High Chamberlain, hah! [*He bumps himself.*] Out of the question, hah! [*He bumps himself again.*] Blue poodles, hah! Hah! I did not forget! Kings never forget! [*Again, he bumps himself.*] Everything gets in my way. I'd better sit down.

[*The* KING *spreads his train and settles his crown. The* WIZARD *enters, down right, very sure of himself, his hand on a list in his pocket. He bows very low.*]

KING [*loftily*]

I want the moon for my little daughter. I expect you to get it.

WIZARD [*taken aback, drawing out a list, hurriedly*]

I have worked a great deal of magic for you in my time, your Majesty. As a matter of fact, I just happen to have in my pocket a list of the wizardries I have performed for you. [*He draws out the list.*] It begins, "Dear Royal Wizard: I am returning, herewith, the so-called philosopher's stone which you claimed——" No, that isn't it! [*He draws out another list from another pocket.*] Here it is. [*He reads.*] "I have squeezed blood out of turnips for you and turnips out of blood. I have produced rabbits out of silk hats and silk hats out of rabbits. I have conjured up flowers, tambourines, and doves out of nowhere and nowhere out of flowers, tambourines, and doves. I have brought you divining rods, magic wands, and crystal spheres in which to behold the future. I have compounded philters, unguents, and potions to cure heartbreak, surfeit, and ringing in the ears. I have made you my own special mixture of wolfbane, nightshade, and eagles' tears to ward off witches, demons, and things that go bump in the night. I have given you seven-league boots, the golden touch, and a cloak of invisibility——"

KING

It didn't work. The cloak of invisibility didn't work.

WIZARD

Yes, it did.

KING

No, it didn't. I kept bumping into things the same as ever.

WIZARD

The cloak is supposed to make you invisible. It is not supposed to keep you from bumping into things.

KING [*shouting*]

All I know is, I kept bumping into things!

WIZARD [*waving his list and reading*]

I got you "horns from elfland, sand from the sandman, and gold from the rainbow." Also——"a spool of thread, a paper of needles, and a lump of beeswax——" Sorry. Those are things my wife wrote down for me to get.

KING

What I want you to do now, is to get me the moon. The Princess Lenore wants the moon, and when she gets it she will be well again.

WIZARD

Nobody can get the moon. It is one hundred thousand miles away, and it is made of green cheese, and it is twice as big as this palace.

[*The* KING *claps his hands in fury, waving the* WIZARD *to the door. The* WIZARD *scurries off, down right, crestfallen.*]

KING

Away with you! Out of my sight! Get back to your cave! Send me the Royal Mathematician! [*He continues, after the* WIZARD *is off.*] Royal Wizard, bah! [*He bumps himself.*] It didn't work! [*He bumps himself again.*] I tell you, the invisible cloak didn't work! [*He strides to sit on the throne, arranging his train and crown.*]

[*The* MATHEMATICIAN *enters, down right, in haste, pulling out his parchment scroll as he comes.*]

KING

I don't want to hear a long list of things you have figured out for me since nineteen-seven! I want to figure out right now how to get the moon for the Princess Lenore. When she gets the moon, she will be well again.

MATHEMATICIAN

I am glad you mentioned the things I have figured out for you since nineteen-seven. [*He pulls the scroll out all the way.*] I have figured out for you the distance between the horns of a dilemma, night and day, and "A" and "Z." I have computed how far is "up," and how long it takes to get "away," and what becomes of "gone." I have discovered the length of the sea serpent, the price of the priceless, and the square of the hippopotamus. I know where you are when you are at "sixes and sevens," and how much "is" you have to have to make an "are," and how many birds you can catch with the salt in the ocean—one hundred and eighty-seven million, seven hundred and ninety-six thousand, one hundred and thirty-two, if it would interest you to know.

KING

There aren't that many birds.

MATHEMATICIAN

I didn't say there were. I said *if* there were.

KING

I didn't want to hear about seven hundred million imaginary birds. I want you to get the moon for the Princess Lenore.

MATHEMATICIAN

The moon is three hundred thousand miles away. It is round and flat, like a coin, only it is made of asbestos, and it is half the size of this kingdom. Furthermore, it is pasted on the sky. Nobody can get the moon.

[*The* KING *jumps to his feet, quivering all over and teetering on his heels.*]

KING

Avaunt! Begone! Get out! And stay out!

[*The* MATHEMATICIAN *drops his pencils over and over in his haste and keeps picking them up as he flees, down right. When he is gone, the* KING'S *rage gradually gives way to anguish. The angry click of his heels fades to silence. His fury subsides to panic-stricken quiet. He stares straight ahead.*]

KING

What will happen to my child if even my Wisemen aren't wise after all?

[*The* KING *rings the tinkling bell and sinks onto his throne, his head in his hands. The* JESTER *comes bounding in, back, and sits at the foot of the throne.*]

JESTER

What can I do for your Majesty?

KING

Nobody can do anything for me. The Princess Lenore wants the moon and she cannot be well till she gets it, but nobody can get it for her. Every time I ask anybody for the moon, it gets larger and farther away. There is nothing you can do for me except to play on your lute. Something sad.

[*The* JESTER *bends over and whispers to the lute. It begins to play softly, the same music. He listens intently, looking far*

off. At an impatient gesture from the KING, *the* JESTER
looks up.]

JESTER

I was just thinking, your Majesty. How big do they say the
moon is and how far away?

KING

The Lord High Chamberlain says it is thirty-five thousand
miles away and bigger than the Princess' bedroom. The
Wizard says it is one hundred thousand miles away and twice
as big as this palace. The Royal Mathematician says it is
three hundred thousand miles away and half the size of this
kingdom.

JESTER [*after listening to the music intently an instant*]

They are all wise men, so they must be right. If they are all
right, then the moon must be just as large and just as far
away as each person thinks it is. The thing to do is to find
out how big the Princess Lenore thinks it is, and how far
away.

KING

I never thought of that.

JESTER

I will go and ask her.

[*The* JESTER *bounds to the door, back, but is stopped by the
voice of the* PRINCESS, *offstage.*]

PRINCESS [*offstage*]

I want a drink of water.

[*The* JESTER *bounds to meet her and brings the* PRINCESS *on,
wavering with weakness.*]

KING

You are too ill to come down all those stairs. You should ring for the Royal Nurse to bring you what you want.

PRINCESS

It makes her say, "Go to sleep." I can't go to sleep till I have the moon. Have you got the moon for me?

JESTER

Not yet, but I will get it right away. How big do you think it is?

PRINCESS

It is just a little smaller than my thumbnail, for when I hold my thumbnail up to the moon, it just covers it.

JESTER

And how far away is it?

PRINCESS

It is not as far away as the top of the big tree outside my window, for last night it got caught in the top branches.

JESTER [*looking out the window*]

Tell me, Princess Lenore, how can the moon be caught in the top branches and not shine in my eyes when I look up at them?

PRINCESS

That is easy, silly. The moon never shines in the daylight. It is too far away. When I hold it in my hand, it will shine all the time.

JESTER

It will be very easy to get the moon for you. I will climb the tree and pick it off the top branches.

PRINCESS

Then I will go to sleep until you bring it, if my father will carry me upstairs.

[*The* KING *picks the* PRINCESS *up, or, if he is not large enough, supports her offstage.*]

JESTER

Wait, your Majesty. What is the moon made of, Princess?

PRINCESS

Oh, it's made of gold, of course, silly.

[*The* KING *and the* PRINCESS *go off, back, and up the stairs. The* JESTER *bounds to the dais and pulls the Goldsmith's bell. He puts his thumb and finger together to make a circle, and experiments with the size he can cover with his thumbnail. The Goldsmith's* DAUGHTER *enters, back.*]

DAUGHTER

Your Majesty, the Goldsmith sent me——Oh! My father thought the King rang to give us an order to make something.

JESTER

I rang. There is something the King wants me to get for the Princess. The Royal Goldsmith must make it immediately, if not sooner.

DAUGHTER

Tell us, and it is done.

JESTER

The Goldsmith must make a tiny round golden piece, and put it on a chain. It must be just large enough to be covered by your thumbnail. [*He illustrates.*]

DAUGHTER [*copying the* JESTER]

So.

JESTER

Your circle is smaller than mine.

DAUGHTER

My thumbnail is smaller than yours.

JESTER

I'm glad you thought of that. It must be just a little smaller than the thumbnail of the Princess Lenore.

DAUGHTER

That will be just a little smaller than mine.

[CYNICIA *and* PARETTA *enter, down right, put their fingers to their lips at the sight of the* JESTER, *nod at each other, and slip where they can listen without being seen.*]

JESTER

String it on a golden chain.

DAUGHTER

We have chains ready.

JESTER

Bring it to me in the garden the instant it is done. The Princess is getting weaker all the time. She will not be well until I get it.

[*The* JESTER *and the Goldsmith's* DAUGHTER *go out, back, she turning right, to the shop, he, left, to the garden.* CYNICIA *and* PARETTA *tiptoe after them a little.*]

CYNICIA

Did you hear what he said?

PARETTA

Yes. What did he mean?

CYNICIA

You can never tell what he means. He's turning something——

PARETTA

—inside out.

CYNICIA

No.

PARETTA

Upside down.

CYNICIA

No! No—*over* in his mind. This court is no place for a trapeze mind.

PARETTA

What do you think the Goldsmith's daughter is to bring him?

CYNICIA

Something on a golden chain.

PARETTA

Something to make the Princess well again.

CYNICIA

That is impossible. She won't be well till she gets the moon.

PARETTA

I know what it is! How dreadful!

CYNICIA

What is it?

PARETTA

A charm to work spells! The Jester has jumped at a way to work magic!

CYNICIA

What would he use magic for?

PARETTA

What will make the Princess well?

CYNICIA

A charm to conjure the moon from the sky!

PARETTA

The Wizard says no one can do that because it is so large.
But it could be done if you had a charm—because as a matter of fact, the moon is only as large as a wagon wheel.

CYNICIA [*very positive*]

The moon is the size of a dinner plate. Husbands always
exaggerate. If the Jester can conjure it out of the sky, he will
cover our husbands with shame.

PARETTA

It will not be the Jester who conjures the moon from the
sky! I will get hold of this charm. I will give it to the
Wizard.

CYNICIA

How can you get it?

PARETTA

Look. [*She holds out a folded cloak she has been carrying.*]

CYNICIA

I don't see anything.

PARETTA

Feel.

CYNICIA [*feeling the cloak*]

Why . . .

PARETTA

It is the invisible cloak the Wizard made for the King. I
have just mended the holes the King tore in it when he
bumped into things. I will wear it to the Goldsmith's shop.
No one will know I am there. [*She puts on the cloak.*]
When the charm is ready, I will steal it away. [*She starts
toward the door, back.*] Tell the Wizard. Bring him here. I
will give it to him.

CYNICIA

I hear your feet. Be sure they do not hear you in the Goldsmith's shop.

PARETTA [*returning*]

Stand outside, where you can't see me. Now, tell me if you can hear me move.

[CYNICIA *goes out, down right.* PARETTA *tiptoes toward the door, and then backs soundlessly toward the other door. The* KING *enters, back, light-footed, joyous that the* PRINCESS *will be well again, and bumps pellmell into* PARETTA'S *retreating rear. She covers her mouth to hold back a scream and stands motionless, fearing to be heard if she moves. The* KING *backs away with a gasp, gets himself together, and tries again with redoubled force. He gives so loud a cry that it covers the sound of her stumble. The* KING *staggers to the dais and pulls the bell cords wildly. He sinks onto the throne, covering his eyes.*]

KING [*to himself, in horror*]

The air went "bump"!

[PARETTA *waves to* CYNICIA, *who is peering into the room, and goes out, back, to the Goldsmith's shop.* CYNICIA *goes out, down right. The* KING *slowly uncovers his face, stares at the place where the collision took place, and shouts.*]

KING

No! I am not afraid! A father is never afraid!

[*At the sound of someone coming, the* KING *assumes great dignity. The* CHAMBERLAIN *enters, down right, followed shortly by* CYNICIA, *ushering in the* WIZARD.]

CHAMBERLAIN

Your Majesty rang?

KING

Something goes "bump" in my throne room.

CHAMBERLAIN

That is out of the question, your Majesty. Nothing goes "bump" in broad daylight. In the nighttime, yes; in the daytime, no.

KING

I was walking across the room, and all of a sudden the air went "bump."

CHAMBERLAIN

I assure you there is no such thing as air going "bump." The ground, yes; the ocean, yes. The air, no.

KING

It might be no such thing yesterday, and yet go "bump" today. What I want of you now is not to tell me what happened didn't happen. I want you to tell me what to do about it! One of you tell me what to do about it! [*He jerks the bell wildly.*] Ask the Royal Mathematician!

[*The* KING *hunches over in despair, holding his clasped hands between his knees, his head bowed, his eyes shut. The* MATHEMATICIAN *hurries in, down right. The* WIZARD *slips over to peer out, back, for his wife, and shows by his attitude that she is coming. In an instant,* PARETTA *enters, back, stealthily, holding the golden chain, with the little round moon hanging on it, up to view. She holds it gingerly, being a little afraid of it. The* WIZARD *looks at it, his head sidewise, also a little afraid of it.* PARETTA *has taken off the cloak.*]

WIZARD [*softly, eyeing the chain*]

Abacadabra. Abacadabra . . .

KING [*looking up*]

Don't stand there muttering magic. Tell me what to do.

PARETTA [*hastily*]

Your Majesty, my husband's power is wonderful. He has just conjured the air in your throne room. It will not go "bump" any more. Try it.

[*The* KING *stares at the spot and very cautiously goes to it, and through it. He is greatly relieved.*]

KING

It is strange, if you can do that, that you could not get the moon for the Princess.

[*The* JESTER *comes bounding into the room, back, from the garden.*]

JESTER

I was playing on my lute in the garden, and all of a sudden it seemed to me the Princess had need of me.

KING

The Princess is sleeping.

JESTER [*lifting a finger*]

Shhh-h-h-h . . .

[*The* OTHERS *obey the* JESTER'S *sign for silence. The music of the moonlight rises softly, coming nearer. Only the* JESTER *hears it. The* OTHERS *look from him to each other, wondering.*]

KING

Do you hear something?

JESTER

The Princess is coming down the marble stairs.

[*The* KING *moves to look out the door.*]

KING

She is asleep. Do not startle her.

[*A happy laugh comes from the* PRINCESS, *offstage. She enters, back, sleepwalking, and talking softly. There is perfect stillness, otherwise, as they watch her. She pauses just short of center stage, and turns, speaking to someone in her dream.*]

PRINCESS

Isn't it funny, Nurse? I was crying for the moon and the Wisemen thought it was only tarts I wanted. The Jester knew. He showed me this shining path I'm walking on. What? [*She pauses, as if listening to someone.*] Can't you see it? I'm walking on a path of light, on the water. I'm going to get my moon. [*She pauses, shaking her head, in disagreement with her imagined speaker.*] What makes you say the moon isn't mine? Of course, it's mine! I like it. What I like is mine. The Jester said so. He said what you like is part of you forever. [*She laughs—a laugh of wonder.*] The moon is part of me. Everything it shines on is part of me. Temples, and animals, and hot lands covered with sand, and cold lands covered with snow and islands, and all the faraway folks. [*She laughs.*] I don't believe the Royal Mathematician could count up all the million, billion, zillion things that are part of me. I'm making up a song about it. It begins:

"I like whatever the moon can see,

And everything under the moon likes me———"

[*There is a burst of laughter from the* WISEMEN *and* PAR-
ETTA *and* CYNICIA. *The sudden loud sound startles the*
PRINCESS *awake. She looks around, dazed, wavers, and
reaches for support. The* OTHERS *start to her, but the* JESTER
is ahead of them all. He seats her on the bench, gently.]

JESTER

It's all right, Princess. You were dreaming.

PRINCESS

Have you brought the moon to me?

JESTER [*looking around anxiously*]

Not yet.

PRINCESS [*growing fainter and fainter*]

You promised me—Father said—the Wisemen—would—
get—the moon.

[*The* PRINCESS *crumples against the* JESTER, *limp, eyes
closed. There is instant hubbub,* EVERYONE *talking at once.*]

KING

Send for the Royal Nurse!

PARETTA [*shaking the* WIZARD *by the arm*]

Use it! Use it!

WIZARD [*examining the chain frantically*]

I don't know how! There are no words on it.

PARETTA

The Princess will die!

WIZARD [*terrified*]

Abacadabra, abacadabra!

MATHEMATICIAN [*walking around*]

A hundred, a thousand, a million, a billion, a trillion!

CYNICIA [*to the* CHAMBERLAIN, *putting his glasses on him*]
Look as if you knew something!

[*Over the sounds comes the voice of the Goldsmith's* DAUGH-
TER, *who enters, back, in great haste.*]

DAUGHTER
Where is the Court Jester?
JESTER [*bounding to her*]
Give me what I ordered. Quick!

[*The* WIZARD *and* PARETTA *show great excitement.*]

DAUGHTER
I had it ready, but when I turned around to pick it up to
bring you, it was gone.

[*The* PRINCESS, *with a little moan, slips down in her chair,
unconscious.* EVERYONE *cries out at once.*]

KING
Lenore!
PARETTA [*to the* WIZARD]
Look at the Princess! Use it! Use it!
WIZARD
I don't know how! There's no writing on it.
JESTER [*calming them with an uplifted hand before he speaks*]
She's only gone away and left herself behind. [*He turns to
the* DAUGHTER.] You must bring it. It will cure her.

[*The* WIZARD *steals near them,* PARETTA *close behind.*]

DAUGHTER
Cure her! What is this that I have made?

[*The* WIZARD *and* PARETTA *wait, ready for their triumph.*]

JESTER

That is the moon. You have made the moon.

[*The* DAUGHTER *steps back, staring, speechless. During her wait, the* WIZARD *lifts the little moon on its chain and turns to* PARETTA.]

WIZARD [*in disgust, very low*]

Magic! Huh! [*He drops it at the feet of the* DAUGHTER *with a gesture of contempt.*]

DAUGHTER [*recovering her tongue*]

But the moon is five hundred thousand miles away, and is made of bronze and is round like a marble.

JESTER

That's what you think. [*He suddenly sees the chain and snatches it up.*] What is this?

DAUGHTER

It must have caught in my skirt!

[*The* JESTER *bounds with the chain to kneel by the* PRINCESS, *takes her limp hand, and puts the chain and tiny moon in it. After a flurry of surprise at his words, the* OTHERS *watch in tense silence.*]

JESTER

Come back, Princess. I have brought you the moon.

[*The* PRINCESS *does not stir. The* KING *wrings his hands in grief.*]

JESTER

It's your funny Jester calling you. I'm wiping the tears away. Open your eyes. Look in your hand.

[*The* PRINCESS *stirs, sighs, opens her eyes, looks at her hand, and then up at the* JESTER. *He takes the chain and holds it up.*]

JESTER

Touch it. It is yours.

PRINCESS

It shines. It is gold. Hold it over there.

[*The* JESTER *steps away, holding it higher than her head. The* PRINCESS *holds up her thumbnail to test the size. She sits up, enchanted.*]

PRINCESS

It's just exactly what I thought it was! [*She rises and goes a little unsteadily to the* JESTER.] Put it around my neck.

[*The* JESTER *puts the chain around the* PRINCESS' *neck.*]

PRINCESS

Now I shall be well again!

KING

I will carry you up to bed, my dear.

PRINCESS

I don't want to go to bed.

[*The* PRINCESS *walks away, very steady. The* OTHERS, *not expecting it, step toward her with steadying hands held out.*]

PRINCESS

You don't have to hold me up any more. I'm strong. I have my moon. [*She stands, glowing, strong.*]

KING

It's almost——

PARETTA

——magic!

KING

I was going to say, beyond belief. I must get to work and practice believing things.

[*The* JESTER *bounds to say a quick word in the* KING'S *ear.*]

JESTER

Have a care what you practice believing, your Majesty.

[*The* JESTER *bounds back to the* PRINCESS *and bows, hands held to his head for rabbit ears, and prances. She claps her hands in delight.*]

PRINCESS

This is the Kingdom of the Rabbits. Every one in this room is a rabbit! The Jester and I are dancing on the seashore. The rest of you are using your paws to clap out the time or pound it out on the ground!

JESTER [*setting the rhythm*]

It goes like this.

PRINCESS

Father must sit on his throne and watch. The rest of you must stand here—[*She indicates a half circle.*]—and clap. Whenever the Jester goes in front of you, you must bow, very low, because he is the wisest of you all. He knew how to get the moon.

CHAMBERLAIN [*widening his eyes*]

I assume this is only in the Kingdom of the Rabbits, your Majesty.

MATHEMATICIAN

It would take me years to figure out the distance between what is and what would be, if it weren't.

WIZARD

Surely your Majesty can't believe his Jester is wiser than his Wisemen.

KING

I never thought of that. It might be a good thing to practice on. Never mind that, now. What I want now is to have the Princess happy.

[*The rhythm starts, and a gay little dance develops. Now and again, the* JESTER, *at the* PRINCESS' *gesture of command, passes before the* WISEMEN, *and they bow low, under the compelling eye of the* KING. *The* PRINCESS *is delighted each time and curtseys to the* JESTER *at the end of the dance.*]

PRINCESS [*overjoyed, as they finish with a flourish*]

I'm all well again! I can play! [*She snatches up a rope which lies on a chair.*] I can even jump my rope! It dropped right out of my hands, I was so tired. [*She turns to the* JESTER.] Come on! Come on, Father! I want to play in the garden!

[*The* PRINCESS *jumps her rope around the stage, followed by the* JESTER, *whirling as they go off, back, past the* KING, *who marches with great strides and no bumping at all. At the door the* KING *turns, and looks the* WISEMEN *up and down.*]

KING [*meditatively*]

I never thought of that.

[*At a burst of laughter from the* JESTER *and the* PRINCESS, *offstage, the* KING *leaves.*]

PARETTA [*to the* WIZARD]

You had it in your hands and didn't know enough to use it!

[PARETTA *and* CYNICIA *go to the window.*]

MATHEMATICIAN

Bowing to the Jester! What's the King doing now?

PARETTA

He's playing with the Princess, like a child.

CHAMBERLAIN

What's the Jester doing?

CYNICIA

Watching.

WIZARD

Has he got that far-off, find-out look?

CYNICIA

No. He's feeling full of himself, because he cured the Princess.

MATHEMATICIAN

How do you know?

CYNICIA

Of course he is. Wouldn't you?

PARETTA

I wish there was some way we could get ahead of him, still.

CYNICIA

There must be something the Jester forgot.

[*The* WISEMEN *pace the floor, upset. The* CHAMBERLAIN *wipes his forehead and blows his nose. The* MATHEMATICIAN *stares at his pencils. The* WIZARD *stares into his cap.*]

CHAMBERLAIN

Where can I send for something the Jester forgot? . . . A mile—a hundred miles—a thousand miles—fifteen thousand—twenty-five thousand—thirty-five thousand——Hah!

[*They* ALL *stop, waiting.*]

CHAMBERLAIN [*putting on his glasses*]

I know what the Jester forgot!

CYNICIA

Tell us.

CHAMBERLAIN

Something thirty-five thousand miles away!

WIZARD [*catching the idea*]

You mean one hundred thousand miles away!

MATHEMATICIAN [*catching it, also*]

You mean three hundred thousand miles away!

PARETTA

You mean the moon!

CYNICIA

Why didn't you say so before?

[*They* ALL *look at each other in triumph, grinning.*]

PARETTA

What will happen when the moon shines in the sky again?

CYNICIA

The Jester won't feel so full of himself.

CHAMBERLAIN

The King will find out who is wise!

[*They* ALL *laugh. The* MATHEMATICIAN *sobers.*]

WIZARD

What is it?

MATHEMATICIAN

The Princess.

WIZARD [*catching his breath*]

What will happen to the Princess Lenore?

CHAMBERLAIN

She will be ill again.

MATHEMATICIAN

She will be very ill.

PARETTA

You must give her your potion to cure heartbreak.

WIZARD

That is to cure not having what you want. To have what your
heart desires and lose it is a different sort of heartbreak. It
takes a very special kind of magic to cure that.

MATHEMATICIAN

What will happen to our Princess when the moon shines in
the sky?

[*They* ALL *stand, very solemn, looking at each other.*]

CURTAIN

ACT THREE

SCENE: *The bedroom of the Princess Lenore. A window, left, half way down, may be the same one used in the other scenes, or a different one, but it is also long and narrow. There is a wide bed, if practical, but if necessary a cot or a low table from one of the schoolrooms may be used. In any case, the royal insignia is at the head of the bed and on a wide, ruffled pillow. There must be no canopy; the pillars of it would block the Princess' face from many places in the audience. A bench stands at the foot of the bed. It, also, may be the same as used before, or it may be covered by a decorated cloth, or be an entirely different one. The bed is right of center stage, parallel with the window, with sufficient space between them to allow the actors free use of the window. There are chairs, down right, and back, by the side of the bed. There is a wide door, back, left, and a narrower one, down right.]*

AT RISE OF CURTAIN: CYNICIA *is standing by the window.* PARETTA *is standing in the wide doorway, back, looking in.]*

CYNICIA

Come and look. You can see the Princess down in the garden. And the Court Jester.

PARETTA [*crossing to the window*]

Is he jumping at conclusions?

CYNICIA

No. He's playing with the Princess.

PARETTA [*with satisfaction*]

Then he hasn't remembered what he forgot.

CYNICIA

Neither has the King. He's walking back and forth, looking at the sunset. He isn't bumping into things.

PARETTA

He isn't trying to keep from remembering. He isn't talking to himself.

CYNICIA

That won't last long. . . . Look!

PARETTA

The rim of the moon! It's peeping over the horizon already.

CYNICIA

It's getting larger every second!

PARETTA

There's a tiny path to it on the water!

CYNICIA

They don't see it.

PARETTA

The garden wall is too high. Pretty soon the moon will rise above the wall and look into the garden.

CYNICIA

The King is going out the garden gate. . . . He's closed it after him.

PARETTA

Look! He's waving his arms about.

CYNICIA

He's bumping into rocks, and things.

PARETTA

He saw the moon.

CYNICIA

What will he think of the Jester now?

PARETTA

There he goes back into the garden. He's rushing into the palace.

CYNICIA

He's shut the gate, so the Princess can't see the moon. He didn't stop to tell the Jester. He'll call our husbands and ask them what to do.

PARETTA

We must warn them. They must feel wiser——

CYNICIA

—and seem wiser——

PARETTA

—and look wiser——

CYNICIA

—and act wiser——

PARETTA

—than they ever did before.

CYNICIA

I hear him on the stairs!

PARETTA [*running to look out the wide door, back*]

He's stopped in his own bedroom.

[*There is the sound of the bell, offstage—three long and one short.*]

CYNICIA

He's calling the Lord High Chamberlain. I must give him something new to do to seem wise. He mustn't wipe his forehead any more, or blow his nose like a trumpet. He did that when the Jester did the thing he couldn't.

PARETTA

The Wizard mustn't look into his cap and say "Abacadabra" any more, either. It did no good. I'll think up something new and surprising for him to do.

CYNICIA

The Mathematician mustn't count any more, either. He couldn't get the moon when he did that. The poor man hasn't any wife to tell him what to do. We must tell him——

PARETTA

—how to seem more wise.

[*Bumping feet are heard on the stairs, and a mumbling voice, offstage.*]

CYNICIA

It's the King, talking to himself. I hope he's calling the Jester names.

[CYNICIA *seizes* PARETTA'S *arm to hurry her off. They whisk out the door, down right, as the* KING *enters, back, talking as he comes. He bumps into the door, and then into the chair by the bed.*]

KING

She'll be ill again. [*He bumps himself.*] What kind of a father am I? [*He bumps himself again.*] It didn't work! [*He shouts.*] That cloak didn't work! Nothing ever works! Everything always gets in my way! [*He is at the window.*] Even the moon in the sky. I can see it move! It will look over the garden wall. Why did I ring for the Lord Chamberlain? He'll only blow his nose, and look through his glasses at me.

[*The* KING *clutches his head in desperation. The* CHAMBER-LAIN *comes to the door, down right.* CYNICIA *is just behind him. She adjusts his glasses. He starts to wipe his forehead, and she snatches the handkerchief away, holds his nose, shakes her head, lets go, and pushes him in.* CYNICIA *disappears as the* CHAMBERLAIN *enters.*]

CHAMBERLAIN

Your Majesty——

[*The* KING *at once assumes regal dignity. He sits on the bench at the foot of the bed.*]

KING

We must keep the Princess from seeing the moon when it shines in the sky tonight. Think of something.

[*The* CHAMBERLAIN, *with a glance toward the door for the approval of his peeping wife, lifts his head, closes his eyes, and taps his forehead thoughtfully. The* KING'S *face brightens with hope.*]

CHAMBERLAIN

I know just the thing. The Royal Wizard can conjure up some dark glasses for the Princess Lenore, in the twinkling of an eye. He can make them so dark she will not be able to see anything at all through them. Then she will not be able to see the moon when it shines in the sky.

[*At the mention of the glasses, the* KING *shakes his head and continues to shake it with more and more violence. The* CHAMBERLAIN *does not see this till he opens his eyes, beaming at the* KING *with pride in his wisdom. Then he*

starts, cowers, takes off his glasses, and retreats before the
KING, *who follows him to the door, shouting.*]

KING

If she wore dark glasses she would bump into things, and
then she would be ill again! What sort of wise man are you?
You might as well be a pigeon, walking on the garden grass,
for all the good you are to me! Send the Royal Wizard here!

[*The* CHAMBERLAIN *goes out, down right. The* KING *hurries to the window, bumping on the bed, and returns to the
bench, to slump onto it, the picture of despair.*]

KING

My child will be ill when she sees the moon, and all I can
do is to bump into things. Kings should not go "bump." I
remember once, how I——[*He leaps up, frantic.*] I will not
remember those things! [*He bumps his way to the window
and looks out, in terror.*] It will soon be shining over the
garden wall and right into the Princess' eyes! [*He shouts.*]
Where is the Wizard?

[*The* WIZARD *has come to the door, down right.* PARETTA *is
straightening his cap and tapping the sides of his head. At
the* KING'S *shout, she pushes the* WIZARD *in.*]

WIZARD

Your Royal Wizard is——

[PARETTA *opens her mouth to say "here," but the* WIZARD'S
*hand over her mouth prevents her. He pushes her out and
finishes his sentence without a break.*]

WIZARD [*continuing*]

—awaiting the King's pleasure.

KING [*more dignified than ever*]

We must hide the moon so the Princess Lenore will not see it shines in the sky tonight. How are we going to do that?

[*The* WIZARD *puts his cap on the bed, a finger on each side of his head in thought. He stands on his hands, then on his feet, then on his head, then on his feet, holding up his cap, and gazing up into it with a great air of mystery. Then he speaks.*]

WIZARD

I know what to do. I have some black velvet curtains in my cave. We can stretch them on poles, at once. The curtains will cover the palace gardens like a circus tent, and the Princess Lenore will not be able to see through them, so she will not be able to see the moon in the sky.

[*At the mention of curtains, the* KING *begins waving the* WIZARD *away. The* WIZARD *does not see this because he is gazing up into his cap. He jumps when the* KING *shouts at him in fury, waving his arms wildly.*]

KING

Black velvet curtains would keep out the air! The Princess would not be able to breathe and she would be ill again! What is the use of a wise man like you? You might as well be a seal in a circus, for all the good you are to the Princess! Send me the Mathematician!

[*The* WIZARD, *hat in hand, starts out, down right.* PARETTA *reaches through the door and puts it on him as he goes out. The* KING'S *fury leaves him so worn out that he wanders about, not noticing that he bumps into the edge of the bed. He looks out the window, groans, and sinks onto the bed, leaning back against the pillow as he talks, despondent, slipping lower and lower.*]

KING

Even my Wisemen think up foolish things. I can't even choose men wise enough to tell me what to do. What the Princess wanted was such a simple thing to get that even my Jester could find it out, but my Wisemen were no help at all. Why did I dream they could tell me how to hide a thing that is so many different sizes and is so many different distances away? I am not fit to be King. I am not fit to be the father of Lenore. I am always doing the wrong thing for her. [*He covers his face with the pillow, with a groan.*]

[*The* MATHEMATICIAN *comes in the door, down right, stares at the* KING, *and then draws himself up, enjoying the surprise he will give him.*]

MATHEMATICIAN

Your Majesty——

[*The* KING *rises, doubly majestic, feeling ashamed that he was caught in such a position.*]

KING [*brusquely*]

We must do something so that the Princess Lenore will not see the moon when it shines in the sky tonight. If you know so much, figure out a way to do that.

[*The* MATHEMATICIAN *walks around in a circle, his body bent, his hands clasped behind his back, his steps longer and longer. Then he straightens and walks around in a square with great dignity. Then he stands still, holding up a pencil.*]

MATHEMATICIAN

I have it! We can set off fireworks in the garden tonight and every night. I have a lot of silver fountains and golden cascades, and when they go off they will fill the garden with so many sparks that it will be as light as day, and the Princess will not be able to see the moon.

[*The* KING *teeters on his heels when the* MATHEMATICIAN *mentions fireworks, and is jumping up and down with anger by the time he finishes.*]

KING

Fireworks would keep the Princess Lenore awake! She would not get any sleep at all and she would be ill again. Don't stand there, looking wise! You might as well be an owl blinking at the sun, for all the good you are to me! Go to the garden and send the Jester here.

MATHEMATICIAN

The Jester!

KING

Yes, the Jester. J-e-s-t-e-r—Jester!

MATHEMATICIAN

Surely, your Majesty can't mean——

KING

I mean the Jester. The Jester! Send me the Court Jester!

MATHEMATICIAN

First, I must figure and count and compute——

[*The* MATHEMATICIAN *starts around in circles, more bent and swift and long-stepped than before. He does not even notice that his circle takes him up on to the bench at the foot of the bed and down again. The* KING *jumps up and down in rage, shouting. The* CHAMBERLAIN, *the* WIZARD, CYNICIA, *and* PARETTA *peer through the door, down right.*]

KING

The Jester! The Jester! The Jester!

MATHEMATICIAN [*at the same time*]

Ten million, twenty million . . . [*He continues to count.*]

[*The* WISEMEN, *at the door, and* CYNICIA *and* PARETTA *enter, approaching the* KING *in protest.*]

WISEMEN, CYNICIA, *and* PARETTA

Your Majesty——

[*They stop short, the* MATHEMATICIAN *on the bench, as the* JESTER *bounds into the room, back.*]

JESTER

Was it the wind blowing, or did I hear the King calling me?

KING [*waving at the* OTHERS]

Send these foolish ones away!

CYNICIA [*very low, in the sudden silence*]

He called you . . . [*She is silent, aghast.*]

PARETTA

. . . foolish.

[*The* KING *snaps his fingers, or claps his hands if this is easier for the actor, at the* JESTER.]

JESTER [*very polite*]

His Majesty gives you leave to go.

[*As they still stand, staring, the* JESTER *whirls to bow to each, as in the rabbit dance. They start to bow in return, jerk themselves up, and stalk off, down right. The* KING *sits on the bench, and the* JESTER *bounds to sit at his feet.*]

JESTER

What can I do for your Majesty?

KING

Nobody can do anything for me. The moon is coming up again. It will shine into the garden very soon, and the Princess will know that it is still in the sky and that she does not wear it on a golden chain around her neck. Play me something on your lute—something very sad—for when the Princess sees the moon, she will be ill again.

[*The* JESTER *flutters his hand over the lute, and listens intently to the music. The* KING *makes a gesture of impatience.*]

KING

I'm waiting.

JESTER

I'm having the thoughts the Princess gives me. . . . What do your Wisemen say?

KING

They can think of no way that will not make the Princess ill.

JESTER [*smiling to himself*]

Your Wisemen know everything. If they cannot hide the moon, it cannot be hidden.

[*The* KING *sighs deeply, rises, and goes to the window. He points out in terror.*]

KING

Look! The moon is already shining into the garden! Who can explain to the Princess how the moon can be shining in the sky when it is hanging on a golden chain around her neck?

JESTER

Who could explain how to get the moon when the Wisemen said it was too far away? It was the Princess Lenore. Therefore, the Princess Lenore is wiser than your Wisemen and knows more about the moon than they do. So, I will ask her.

KING [*still at the window, fairly tearing his hair*]

I cannot see the Princess anywhere! She has seen the moon. She is ill again. She is lying weak and alone in some dark shadow!

PRINCESS [*offstage, approaching*]

Where is my dear funny Jester? I am tired of waiting all alone.

KING

She will see it out the window!

JESTER

I will ask her.

KING

Wait! A cloud has covered the face of the moon! Don't say a word to her about it! We'll get her to sleep before the cloud passes and lets the moon shine into her bedroom here. The Princess must hide the moon from herself, behind her own eyelids.

PRINCESS [*nearer, offstage*]

I want my Jester.

JESTER

Here he is!

[*The* JESTER *bounds out, back.*]

KING [*rubbing his hands in satisfaction*]

I'm a little wise, after all. I've found a way to put it off.

[*The* JESTER *and the* PRINCESS *run on, back, laughing. She runs to pull at her father's hand.*]

PRINCESS

Night is coming down, Father, and my moon is filling all the garden with a magic sort of light. Come and see.

KING

Not tonight, Princess. You must go to sleep, right away.

PRINCESS [*dancing away from the* KING]

Why, Father! I'm not ill any more. I have my moon. I haven't time to go to sleep. We must finish our game in the garden.

KING

It's bedtime.

PRINCESS

It's the nicest game the Jester ever made up for me. It's about hiding things from yourself, with your own thumbnail. We'll show you.

KING [*anxiously, at the window*]

Tomorrow.

PRINCESS [*too eager to be stopped*]

Father! I'm showing you our game! [*She illustrates.*] First, I must shut one eye. Now, if I stand here and hold my thumb out as far as I can in front of the other eye, I don't hide but part of you. Now, watch! The closer I bring my thumbnail to my eye, the more of you I hide. Now! I don't see you at all! You might as well be a piece of the dark, for all I see. And yet you're there all the time! Try it, Father. [*She runs to the window.*] See that cloud out there? The one with the bright edges? It is just about as big as I am. [*She takes the* KING's *thumb and lifts it up.*] Now. Can you still see the edges shine?

KING [*nervously*]

Yes. Yes.

PRINCESS

Now, bring your thumbnail closer—closer—closer. Doesn't it hide the cloud now, edges and all?

KING

Yes. [*He speaks loudly.*] But it's still there! [*He is gentle again.*] Come away from the window, Princess. I'm waiting to tuck you into bed.

PRINCESS

I'm not sleepy, Father. There's lots more to our game. We wink at each other.

KING [*clutching his head and sinking onto the bench*]

I can't even keep my own child safe in bed.

[*The* PRINCESS *looks at the* KING, *sorry. She goes to him, full of love, and pats his shoulder.*]

PRINCESS

Don't feel bad, Father. I'll be good. I'll go to bed.

[*The* KING *leaps up and hurries between the bed and the window, with a fearful glance outside. He opens the covers.*]

KING

I'll tuck you in.

[*The* JESTER *bounds over to kneel, and the* PRINCESS *steps from his knee to the bed. She sits up against the great ruffled pillow.*]

KING

Give me your crown and the moon. I'll take care of them.

PRINCESS [*clutching the chain*]

Oh, no! I'll be ill again without my moon. I'll be very ill this time, because I'm all used to having it.

KING [*with a distracted look over his shoulder*]

Lie down, then. I'll tuck the covers around you.

PRINCESS

Not yet. [*She holds her thumb up toward the cloud, out-side.*] The bright edge is getting wider. . . . Now, I'm hiding part of it. . . . Now, it's all gone. Isn't it funny, Father, what big things you can hide from yourself with your own thumbnail?

KING

Lie down, my dear. Shut your eyes.

PRINCESS

First, we must finish our game. We were playing with a flower when you called the Jester. I must be looking at the flower. I can see it from the window if I look down.

[*The* PRINCESS *starts to her knees, to get up. The* KING *holds her back.*]

KING

No, no! You promised to go to bed.

PRINCESS

Then, of course, I can't get up. . . . I know what we can do! I looked at that flower a long time in the garden. I can see it right behind my eyelids when I shut my eyes! So we can finish our game.

KING

Shut them tight.

[*During the following, the* KING *watches the cloud in great panic, moving to cut off from the* PRINCESS *a ray of light which now and then comes in the window. This can be done with a flashlight, if the round moon described in the "Property Plot" is not practical for any given group.*]

PRINCESS

I'll tell you about the flower. When the gardener used his scythe in that part of the garden, he mowed down everything except one flower. That's the one our game's about. I hide it with my thumb and the Jester asks——Show him.

JESTER

What are you hiding from yourself with your thumbnail?

PRINCESS

And I tell him everything that's part of the flower—like, stem, leaves, flower cup, green of the leaves, blue of the flower, roots——

KING

You can't see the root when you look at the flower.

PRINCESS [*clapping her hands*]

You're caught! The root is part of the flower just the same, isn't it?

KING

Yes, I guess it couldn't grow without a root.

PRINCESS

That's the game. Everything means more than you think it does. If I forget something, the Jester remembers. He winks at me. If I can't think of it before he wags his finger three times—[*She wags her finger.*]—so—it's his turn. Now, we'll show you.

JESTER

You can't see me wink with your eyes shut.

KING [*hastily*]

You can tell her when you wink.

PRINCESS

Of course, silly. You can say, "wink, wink, wink!" Ready?

JESTER

We stopped at "root." What else were you hiding from yourself with your thumbnail?

PRINCESS

The sap that comes up from the root. The honey in the flower cup.

JESTER

Wink, wink, wink! The bees and the butterflies and the hummingbirds that drink the honey—the seeds that grow when the honey is gone——

PRINCESS

Wink! The winds that blow the seeds away. The other flowers that grow from the seeds——

JESTER

Wink, wink! All the flowers that grow from them. The children everywhere that pick the flowers, the artists who paint them, the people who write music about them——

PRINCESS

Wink, wink, wink! The sky the flowers look up to all over the world——

JESTER

Wink, wink, wink! The sun that calls them up out of the ground, the day that gives them light, the night that folds the dark around them, the stars that twinkle secrets to them, the moon that fills their cups with a magic sort of light——

PRINCESS

Wink, wink, wink, wink, wink, wink! Everything the moon shines on.

[*The music begins, very softly. The* JESTER *hears it; the* KING *does not. The* PRINCESS *is getting sleepy.*]

PRINCESS

Places I have never seen—temples and gardens and mountains—[*She speaks dreamily.*]—and valleys and rivers and waterfalls—[*She is almost asleep.*]—and other Princesses who live in other lands—and children who are not Princesses—and their fathers, and their mothers—and friends—and enemies . . . [*She stirs, uneasily, her smile fading.*]

JESTER [*bounding to bend low over her, and speaking softly*]
And a flower——

PRINCESS [*her smile returning*]
And the but—ter—flies—that . . . [*Her voice trails to silence. Her face is toward the window; her smile full of peace.*]

KING [*grateful*]
She is asleep.

[*The music fades as they speak. The* KING *comes away from the window without a bump.*]

KING

The cloud has kept my Princess well again.

JESTER

Have you thought about tomorrow?

KING

I will think up something else by then.

JESTER

I will ask the Princess. She is the one to tell us.

KING

No! No! [*He bumps on the bench.*] She will be ill again.

[*The* PRINCESS *stirs.*]

KING

I can't stay here. Things get in my way. I'll waken her. Come with me. Play something on your lute while I watch the cloud that kept her safe. Something very glad and grateful, because the Princess is well again.

[*The* KING *and the* JESTER *tiptoe out, back, their backs to the window, so they do not see that a bright moonbeam has fallen across the bed and is moving toward the* PRINCESS' *face. It falls across her eyes just as they disappear. She stirs, moves her head, and finally turns on her side, back to the moon. She opens her eyes. She sees the light on her hand, and lifts up her moon as far as the chain permits, laughing softly. The* JESTER *peeps into the room, and then enters. The moonlight is streaming into the room by now.*]

JESTER [*seeming very sad*]

Tell me, Princess Lenore. How can the moon be shining in the sky when it is hanging on a golden chain around your neck?

PRINCESS

That is easy, silly. When I lose a tooth, a new one grows in its place, doesn't it?

JESTER

Of course! And when the unicorn loses a horn in the forest, a new one grows in the middle of his forehead.

PRINCESS

That is right. And when the Royal Gardner cuts the flowers in the garden, other flowers come to take their place.

[*The* PRINCESS *closes her eyes, drowsily, smiling. The music rises again, very soft. The* PRINCESS' *voice trails away.*]

PRINCESS

I guess—it is the same—with everything. . . .

[*The* JESTER *straightens the covers, tucking the* PRINCESS *in gently. Then he sits, down right, facing the window and listening to the music with his "far-off, find-out look." Suddenly, the light from the window flickers twice. The* JESTER *starts, looks at the window, and stares ahead of himself.*]

JESTER [*slowly, incredulously, awed*]

It seemed to me the moon winked at me. [*He goes very silently to the window to look up at the moon. His voice is hushed, tremulous, as he winks at the moon.*] Wink, wink . . .

[*There is a repeated flicker of light, or a definite wink from a full moon, whichever the producer is using. The* JESTER *turns to stare straight ahead of him, a glimmer of laughter coming into the awe and wonder which floods his face. It is effective, but not necessary, to dim all other lights at this point and leave only the moonlight on the faces of the* PRINCESS *and the* JESTER.]

CURTAIN

Production Notes

CYNICIA: She is the wife of the Lord High Chamberlain, and is always finding fault with her husband and telling him what to do. This is because she wants him to be the most important man in the King's court, so she will be the most important woman. This makes her a bit thin and tired looking.

THE ROYAL NURSE: She does her very best and knows all about the Princess' temperature and pulse and tongue, but she doesn't know that the little Princess, like every other child, has dreams and longings of her own which are as important to her health as her pulse.

THE LORD HIGH CHAMBERLAIN: He is a large fat man who wears thick glasses. He wants very much to be as important in the eyes of the King as his wife wants him to be, so he uses his glasses to make himself look wise, and sends very far away to get things to astonish the King. He thinks the farther he sends, the more the King will think of him.

PARETTA: She is the wife of the Wizard, and is one of those people who can't wait for others to finish sentences. This is because she is more interested in her own thoughts than in those of other people, so it doesn't matter to her whether she finishes their sentences as they meant to or not. She is always pleased with herself when she finishes a sentence, and beams at others whether they like it or not.

THE ROYAL WIZARD: He is a little thin man with a long face. He wears a high, red-peaked hat covered with silver stars and a long blue robe covered with golden owls. He really can do a little magic, but he pretends he can do more than he can. This is because he is afraid the King will not think he is wise if he knows there is anything he can't do. When he is worried he looks into his peaked hat and says "abacadabra" very fast, to remind himself that he is a great wizard.

THE ROYAL MATHEMATICIAN: He is bald-headed and near-sighted, with a skull cap on his head, and pencils behind his ears. He wears a black suit with white numbers on it, so he can always have some numbers to look at. He is happy when he is adding or subtracting or making a list, but anything that can't be measured, makes him feel mixed up and frightened. Then he walks around and counts very fast. It makes him feel as if he were thinking.

THE PRINCESS LENORE: She loves to laugh and play, but there is something her heart desires so much that she can't be well and strong without it. She can't explain it to the grown-ups because, like every other child, she has feelings she doesn't understand herself; but when the foolish Wisemen give her tarts instead of the moon, she falls very ill, and when the Jester gets the moon for her, she is well and strong again.

THE COURT JESTER: He is so sure that everything will be all right if he just thinks of the right thing, that he is never afraid, and comes bounding in and out to see what he can do for people. He is the only grownup who knows how to play with the Princess. This is because he can forget all about himself and keep perfectly still, till what is happening in her comes to him like music. He has taught his lute to remember what he hears, so he can go on listening to it until it tells him what to do. He wears motley and a cap and bells.

THE KING: He is not a happy man. He tries to act majestic, as a king should, before people, but he is always bumping into things. This is because he secretly feels that he is not all that a king should be, and, worse, that he is not a good father to Princess Lenore, who is the apple of his eye. When he is alone, he walks about and talks out loud to keep from remembering how he feels about himself. Yet that is often the very thing he talks to himself about.

THE GOLDSMITH'S DAUGHTER: She is young and pretty and clever for her age. She knows all about her father's work and does a great deal of it for him. She likes to answer her father's bell, so she can get away from the shop and see the people of the court for a little while.

SUGGESTIONS FOR DIRECTING CHILDREN

The play permits a wide variety of production plans. It may be produced in curtains, or screens, or in a more or less complete setting, as desired. Children will often enjoy designing and making panels or hangings, painted on paper or cloth. Children from the sixth grade, up, who find a manual training or art teacher ready to cooperate, are fascinated with building screens or flats, painting them, and playing with lights. If the play is done by adults for children, their designers and technicians will find unusual opportunity for imaginative use of color and light. In any case, the effect should be simple, to fit the quality of Thurber's story.

The tryout at the Hessville community summer project found high school students eager to design, build, and paint scenery, and design and make costumes for the elementary school actors, under the leadership of an artist. The University of Washington tryout used university students and technicians, of the drama department.

CASTING: Of course the value of the experience to the child is the first consideration in casting, and the ability of the child to imagine a given character is the second; but other things being equal, this play will have greater appeal to an audience if the Princess is the smallest child in the cast, the King is the largest, and the Jester the most agile. Telling the story briefly and vividly and letting the children play freely in different rôles in scenes of their choice, for a while, often works well in fitting the right part to each child.

MEMORIZING: Children are often eager to take their lines home and learn them the first thing. This makes two kinds of trouble. They are apt to learn empty words and bad readings, which they rattle off with little or no reference to others on the stage. Also, they are apt to be "helped" by a grownup who treats the lines as an end in themselves because he does not understand that *a play is not words. It is things that happen between people.*

It takes more time to correct these bad habits, once they are set, than to see that the young actors use their lines to show the audience what they feel and do and why they feel and do it. Once the children feel free to contribute, their amazingly fertile imaginations and their combined backgrounds of experience will start this process, and questions and explanations from the director will fill it in.

It is thrilling to watch a child's imagination seize his voice and body, once it is aroused. In the tryout at the Hessville Community Children's Theatre, the two wives entered, in Act Two, stiff and self-conscious. The director murmured, "They're feeling sly." As one person, they darted behind a nearby table and crouched, the embodiment of eavesdroppers. It is amazing to find how many unexpected explanations come out of a children's cast. In this same tryout the director came to the rehearsal of the sleepwalking scene in Act Two, ready to explain everything. At her very first question: "How do you think you would be walking, Princess?"—one of the boys piped up: "I can show you. My brother walks in his sleep." He not only "showed them," but saw that every one of the interested group could do it, and were duly impressed with his mother's fear of waking him up suddenly. The outbreak of illustrations of the way rabbits leap and twist around and pound on the ground was less unexpected, but no less useful.

It is especially useful to a director of children to keep in mind the things that control memory. They are, in order of their importance: *Intensity of impression,* which means that lines are readily remembered when the meaning and emotion are felt by the actor; *Association,* which means that interaction with others on the stage, movements, positions, meanings, and emotions, should be pretty well set before memorizing is required or even allowed, outside of rehearsal; *Intention to Remember,* which means that in passages where feeling is high or action swift, the lines can be discarded for a bit, after a quick, concentrated look at them; and last of all, *Repetition,* which means that when the time has come, drill at home or in rehearsal is useful in making memory unshakable.

It is usually wise for the director to collect the lines at the end of rehearsal for a time. Each child may be allowed to take his home for drill, when readings and action show that the play has come alive to him.

LISTENING: Good listening is, of course, part of good memorizing. From the very first rehearsal, children can be made to understand that what they feel and do when others are talking and moving is just as important as their own lines, and, indeed, often more so. It is often useful to let them put their reactions into words between rehearsals.

CUES: Good cues are, of course, part of good listening. Children who are not really listening, wait until they hear the last word of the previous speech before they get ready to speak. If they are really listening, however, they will usually hear something earlier in the line which starts the thought expressed in their own line, and be ready to speak without pause. In the few cases in which there is no such "thought cue" ahead of the word cue at the end of the sentence, it is often useful to let the actor repeat the last few words with the other speaker and go on into his own line without pause, until he gets the feeling of a quick cue. It may take a little playful drill to get a quick cue without hurrying the line. Trying to see who can get in first, without actually cutting the preceding line, and yet keep his own line slow, is a game children enjoy. Good cues are worth the time they take, because slow cues cut the value of important pauses. Children can understand the rule: *No pause without a meaning to the audience.*

MOVEMENT: Children find it hard, at first, to stand still. They fidget. They want to move every time they speak. The first is best corrected, not by "Stand still" orders, but by developing good listening. The second is best corrected by giving them the rule: *No movement without a meaning.* Every gesture or step must tell what a character is thinking or feeling. But some movements which are honestly part of a character must be cut out, because too many movements confuse an audience. It is often useful to let those not on the stage sit in various parts of the audience space, to see whether the story is easy to follow.

SENSE OF THE AUDIENCE: It is important to build the right sense of the audience into rehearsals very early. If the actors are vividly conscious of the need to make everything plain to the watchers, and to share the fun and excitement of the story with them, they will neither be afraid of them, nor (what is even worse) be tempted to show off before them. This constant reference to the audience is easy in settling positions ("If you move over a little the audience can see how frightened the King is," or "If you look out a little above the last seat, every one can see how wonderful you think it is that the moon winked at you."). It is easy in correcting readings ("Which idea is it most important for the audience to understand?"), in eliminating unnecessary movement ("Where do you want the audience to look, now?"), and in timing ("Let's give the audience a little more time to enjoy this."), etc.

THE LONG SPEECHES: The speeches of the Wisemen in Act Two may frighten some child actors at first sight. If the child feels that he may choose what items he will keep, and is allowed to ad lib to keep going without any sense of failure, he will end by keeping them all, especially if the humor and background in fairy-lore and history are explained to him. A story hour or two for this purpose will delight the cast. It is quite possible to let the actor print the list on his scroll, separating the items into groups—i.e., color—black orchids, blue poodles, pink elephants, and goldbugs; or instruments of magic—divining rods, magic wands, and crystal spheres. He should know the lines, just the same, so as not to be tied too closely to his list. Making the list will help him learn it, as well as easing his mind. Even more freedom can be allowed the Jester in what he sees when he listens to the Princess' music, and the Wisemen in their list of tarts.

ADJUSTING TO AUDIENCE AGE LEVEL: The younger the children in the audience the shorter their attention span. The play is so written that attention in a child audience is relaxed at definite intervals by large movement, laughter, etc., which do not require attention to lines, and allow movement and noise in the audience without stopping the play. These "anti-exhaustion" spots in the play, like the rabbit dance, the Wizard's standing on his head, the King's rages, etc., can be shortened for older children and lengthened for younger ones. Every director should study the attention span of his audiences, as well as those of his actors, and adjust rehearsal and performance to them. Also, the play has kept many of the "adult overtones" of Thurber's story, which do not stop the action for the children but do give the grownups something to think about. If parents and teachers are expected in number, it is a good idea to remind the child actors: "The grownups will laugh at this."

THE COMEDY: Children love to laugh. Many directors are tempted by the vociferous response of a child audience to carry comedy scenes to an extreme which stops the story. The scene itself is a tremendous success, but the play as a whole suffers, as when, for example, a comic drill of characters going to the rescue of a fallen heroine was so funny and so prolonged that when the poor heroine was finally discovered, a child in the audience asked: "Who is that girl? How did she get there?" In "Many Moons," both the Wisemen and the King may tempt an actor to such over-emphasis of comedy traits. The Wisemen must not be so funny that the audience forgets their great desire to impress the King or loses the point of the scene, which is that the Wisemen cannot get the moon. The King's bumping must not be so funny that the audience forgets the cause of it—his unhappy feeling that he is not a proper king or a good father. Care that he shows his anxiety before he begins to bump will keep this clear. Sharp distinction in his manner when he is alone and when he is before others will help, also. The comedy,

84

like the music and the dancing, is to be controlled by the funda-
mental rule of a play for children: *The story must never stop.*
Comedy for the sake of the story is invaluable. Comedy for its
own sake is bad.

THE RABBIT DANCE

Almost any group of children will have one or two who are
full of the way somebody's rabbits behave, and with a little
help can create a dainty and comic dance. If no such information appears in the cast, it is easy to develop a dance with a
few pictures and the necessary information. Let the "Rabbit"
use his hands for ears; let him alternate hopping, dignified
court steps, and pounding on the floor with his feet; and once,
at least, go on all fours. Any clapped rhythm that fits what develops is usable. For example: Hop—step, step, step, step; bow
—hop, hop, hop, hop; step—pound, pound, pound, pound; all
fours—hop, turn, hop, turn; etc.

Adult actors will of course want to do something more com-
plex and may have to be restrained from making the dance too
long. It is in the text to provide a brief interval of laughter and
large movement, but it must not be overdone. A skilled dance
teacher will find it a delightful medium and may also need to
be warned not to swamp the story with charming dance detail.
The point that the Princess is now well enough to take delight
in making the discomfited Wisemen bow to the Jester must not
be lost sight of. It is better not to use music, if the clapping
can be made satisfactory. The "Moonlight Sonata" should be the
only music in the play.

THE MUSIC

The easiest way to handle the music is to use a recording of
Beethoven's "Moonlight Sonata." In some cases, however, the

director may prefer to use a pianist, with or without a violin accompaniment; in others, humming by a small group or even by a school chorus. However it is produced, only a small portion of the opening section of the sonata is needed to cover the speeches. The music easily lends itself to spacing the lines spoken to it. In the Hessville tryout a sixth-grade child took charge of this with great enthusiasm. "When I get louder," he said to the Jester, "you see the next picture. When I get soft again, you speak." If there is no volume control on the Victrola, the pauses and lines can be placed by phrases in the music. The music begins each time after the Princess (or Jester) has closed eyes, and stops instantly when the day-dream is interrupted.

PROPERTY PLOT

ACT ONE

GENERAL:

Five bell cords.

A long table, with a cover coming to the floor. This may need to have a platform back of it if the play is given by young children, as the action back of the table may be blocked by the table itself.

Two benches.

Chair with high back, and royal insignia at top.

Pyramid of tarts. This may be a cutout, painted to represent a mound of tarts. Corrugated pasteboard, or wallboard, will be satisfactory. Its own support may be fastened to it, or it may have a flap at the bottom which is turned under to hold a pile of books, or any other easy-to-find support.

Other chairs as desired.

CHAMBERLAIN:

Glasses, which are a large frame without lenses, as lenses would reflect light into the eyes of the audience; list of tarts, which he has in his pocket on entrance; a small tart, which is behind the pyramid, which he carries to the Princess; handkerchief.

NURSE:

Thermometer, watch, broken tart in front of the Princess' chair.

CYNICIA:

Same broken tart on plate in front of the Princess' chair.

WIZARD:

Potion in a little bottle, brought on in his hand; a small tart, which he takes from behind the pyramid and carries to the Princess.

MATHEMATICIAN:

A long narrow scroll with list of kinds of tarts; pencils behind each ear (Since several go behind each ear, they had better be artificial and very light. They can well be of bright colors.); small tart, behind pyramid, which he carries to the Princess.

PRINCESS:

Broken tart, on plate in front of her chair.

JESTER:

Lute.

OFFSTAGE:

Record of Beethoven's "Moonlight Sonata."

ACT TWO

GENERAL:

Five bell cords.

Dais for King's throne (if desired).

Throne for the King.

Two benches.

Other chairs as desired.

CHAMBERLAIN:

Scroll from which he reads his list, glasses, handkerchief.

WIZARD:

Two scrolls, one in each pocket.

MATHEMATICIAN:

Scroll from which he reads his list, pencils.

PARETTA:

The invisible cloak, folded (It is effective, but not necessary, to have it of transparent material.); the little gold moon on a chain.

PRINCESS:

Jumping rope, little gold moon on a chain.

JESTER:

Lute.

OFFSTAGE:

Record of "Moonlight Sonata."

ACT THREE

GENERAL:

Bed for the Princess. (It may be a wide bed, or a cot, or a low table from one of the schoolrooms. At the head is the royal insignia.)

Pillow, large, with ruffles.

Bench, at foot of the bed.

Chairs, by door, down right, and near the bed, back.

CHAMBERLAIN:

Glasses, handkerchief.

MATHEMATICIAN:

Pencils.

PRINCESS:

Little moon on a chain.

KING:

Pillow, covers to tuck around the Princess.

JESTER:

Lute.

OFFSTAGE:

Record, "Moonlight Sonata"; bell; moon, or flashlight. The face of a moon can be drawn on a large piece of transparent paper. It is attached to a round frame and then slowly raised in front of the window. A light is placed behind it, which can be snapped on and off when the moon "winks."

STAGE CHARTS

ACT ONE

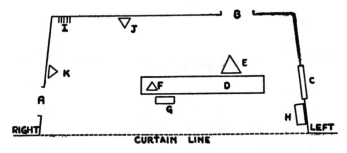

A. Door to the Wisemen's quarters.
B. Door to stairs to Princess' bedroom; back, up the stairs; left, as you go out, to the garden; right, to the Goldsmith's shop.
C. Window overlooking the garden.

D. Table. Two tables from the schoolroom may be put together if a long one is not available. The cloth hangs to the floor. If actors are small, platforms may be needed back of the table.

E. The Princess' chair. The insignia at the top can be on pasteboard and fastened to the back of the chair.

F. Pyramid of tarts. It may be a cutout from pasteboard, and painted to show the many tarts with different colored fillings.

G. Bench.

H. Jester's bench.

I. Cords for King to pull, to call the Wisemen, Jester, etc.

J. Chair, if desired.

K. Chair, if desired.

ACT TWO

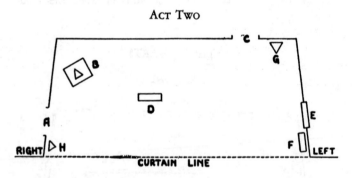

A. Door.

B. Dais for King's throne. The dais is optional. The bell cords can be in the same position as in Act One, or placed elsewhere in the room.

C. Door.

D. Bench.

E. Window.

F. Bench.

ACT THREE

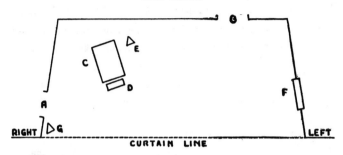

A. Door.

B. Door.

C. The Princess' bed.

D. Bench.

E. Chair.

F. Window overlooking garden.

G. Chair.

Directors write us about

MANY MOONS

"The play is for the children as well as for adults, and can be very delightful to both. The children laughed especially at the Wizard and Lord High Chamberlain and the King. They liked the reading of the list, the Wizard's standing on his head and the characterization in general."—Donna Lee Schmidt, Normal, Ill.

"I think Charlotte Chorpenning's dramatization of James Thurber's 'Many Moons' is an excellent one. The lines are well chosen and the dramatic elements interesting. . . . The children in the audience were delighted with the play."—Vivian E. Burton, Fuquay Springs High School, Fuquay Springs, N. C.

"Having done several other plays with 7th and 8th grade level, I would like to state that 'Many Moons' was the most satisfactory to both director and cast. I anticipate directing it again when opportunity affords. For me it contains limitless possibilities, giving credit to Mr. Thurber's magnificent lines, of course. Thurber's lines afford thought for any mentality, from six to sixty. It was described as being intellectually entertaining as well."—Sister M. Elizabeth Ann, F.S.P.A., Holy Family School, Ashland, Wis.

MANY MOONS

"We had an average of seven curtain calls each show, a great deal of comments on how well the show went, and what a wonderful play 'Many Moons' was for a choice. After each show, people swarmed the stage and asked me if we might do the show again in the future. We had packed houses every performance, and some people came to see it twice. Each member of the cast was very thrilled with his part. All I can say is, 'They loved it!' "—Bob C. LeFeuvre, China Lake Players, China Lake, Calif.

"Wonderful! Our child audiences were so enthralled they scarcely breathed through the entire performance, and the adults loved it even more, if possible. We had four sell-out performances and were promptly asked to give repeat performances this month and next. The cast had the time of their lives. We used adults in the roles, and they created magnificent characterizations."—Margaret Moore, Weathervane Community Theatre, Akron, Ohio.

"Very good."—Margaret Earl McConnell, Oakland City College, Oakland City, Ind.